Tashi and the Giants
© Text, Anna Fienberg and Barbara Fienberg 1995
© Illustrations, Kim Gamble 1995
First published in 1995 by Allen & Unwin Pty Ltd., Australia

大喜說故事系列

Tashi
and the
BANDITS
大喜與強盜

Anna Fienberg
Barbara Fienberg 著

Kim Gamble 繪

王秋瑩 譯

三民書局

One night Jack was reading a book with his father.

'This story **reminds** me of the time Tashi was **captured** by some bandits,' said Jack.

有一天晚上，傑克和老爸一塊兒看書。

「這個故事讓我想起有一回大喜被幾個強盜捉住的事，」傑克說。

remind [rɪ`maɪnd] 勔 使想起

capture [`kæptʃɚ] 勔 捕捉

'Oh good, another Tashi story,' said Dad. 'I suppose Tashi finished up as the Bandit **Chief**.'
'No, he didn't,' said Jack. 'It was like this. One wet and windy night a **band** of **robbers** rode into Tashi's village. They were looking for some **shelter** for the night.

「哦，好耶，另一個大喜的故事，」老爸說。「我猜大喜最後當上了強盜頭頭！」

　　「不，他沒有，」傑克說。「事情是這樣的。在一個風雨交加的夜晚，一群強盜騎馬闖進了大喜的村子。他們正在尋找晚上落腳的地方。

chief [tʃif] 名 首領
band [bænd] 名 一夥
robber [ˋrabɚ] 名 強盜
shelter [ˋʃɛltɚ] 名 棲身之處

'But next morning, just as they were leaving, the wife of the Bandit Chief saw Tashi. He reminded her of her son, who had **sailed** away on a **pirate** ship, and she said to her husband, "That boy looks just like our son, Mo Chi. Let's take him with us."

「不過，隔天早上，就在他們要離開的時候，強盜頭頭的老婆看見了大喜。大喜讓她想起坐上海盜船航海去了的兒子，於是她跟她老公說，『那小子長得好像我們兒子——摩奇。我們把他帶走。』

sail [sel] 動 航行
pirate [`paɪrət] 名 海盜

'So Tashi was picked up and thrown on to one of the horses and away they went. He **sneaked** a good look about him, but he was **surrounded** by bandits, and it was impossible to **escape**. So Tashi had to think up one of his **cunning** plans.

「大喜就這樣被抓起來、丟上馬背，被帶走了。他偷偷地打量著四周，他被強盜團團圍住，是不可能逃跑了。大喜得想個妙法子才行。

sneak [snik] 動 偷偷地做…
surround [sə`raʊnd] 動 包圍
escape [ɪ`skep] 動 逃走
cunning [`kʌnɪŋ] 形 狡猾的

'The first night when the bandits were still sitting around the fire after their dinner, the Bandit Chief said to Tashi, "Come, boy, sing us a song as Mo Chi did, of **treasure** and pirates and fish that shine like **coins** in the sea."

「第一天晚上，強盜們吃完晚餐後，圍著營火靜靜地坐著，強盜頭頭對大喜說，『來，小子，像摩奇一樣唱首寶藏、海盜和魚在海裡像錢幣一樣閃閃發亮的歌來聽聽。』」

treasure [`trɛʒɚ] 名 寶藏

coin [kɔɪn] 名 錢幣

'Tashi saw that this was his **chance**. So what do you think he did?'

'Sang like a **nightingale**,' said Dad.
'Wrong!' said Jack. 'He sang like a **crow**. The bandits all covered their ears and the Bandit Wife said, "Stop, stop! You sing like a crow.

「大喜知道機會來了。你想他怎麼做？」

「唱得像夜鶯那麼美妙，」老爸說。

「錯了！」傑克說。「他唱得跟烏鴉一樣難聽。強盜全搗住了耳朵，強盜婆子大叫，『停，停！你唱得跟烏鴉一樣難聽。

chance [tʃæns] 名 良機

nightingale [ˋnaɪtɪŋˌgel] 名 夜鶯

crow [kro] 名 烏鴉

You had better come over here and **brush** my
hair like my son used to do." Tashi bowed
politely but as he stepped around the fire, he
filled the brush with **thistles** and **burrs** so
that soon her hair was full of **tangles**.

"'Stop, stop!" cried the Bandit Wife, and her
husband told her, "This boy is not like our son.
He sings like a crow and he tangles your hair."
Tashi put on a **sorrowful** face. "I will do better
tomorrow," he promised.

你最好過來這兒像我兒子一樣幫我梳梳頭。」大喜很有禮貌地鞠了躬，不過就在他走到營火附近的時候，他把梳子塞滿了薊和刺果，讓她的頭髮全都纏在一起。

　　「『停，停啊！』強盜婆子大叫，她老公對她說，『這小子不像我們兒子。他唱歌唱得像烏鴉一樣難聽，又讓妳的頭髮打結。』大喜做了一個難過的表情。『我明天會做得更好的，』他保證。

brush [brʌʃ] 動 梳

thistle [`θɪsl̩] 名 薊（有刺植物）

burr [bɝ] 名 刺果類植物

tangle [`tæŋɡl̩] 名 糾纏

sorrowful [`sɑrofəl] 形 悲傷的

"'You'd better," whispered the Chief's brother, Me Too, "or I'll boil you in snake oil."

「『你最好這樣，』強盜頭頭的弟弟密圖低聲地說，
『否則我把你丟到蛇油裡煮一煮。』

'The next day when the bandits moved camp, they put all the rice into three big bags and gave them to Tashi to carry. When they came to a river, what do you think Tashi did?'

'Well,' said Dad, **scratching** his **chin**, 'he's such a clever boy, I expect he carried them over one by one, holding them up high.'

「第二天強盜們拔營的時候，他們把全部的米裝進三個大袋子裡，要大喜背。當他們來到了河邊的時候，你想大喜做了什麼？」

　　「嗯，」老爸搔著下巴說，「大喜那麼聰明，我想他會把袋子舉得高高地，一袋接一袋扛過河。」

scratch [skrætʃ] 動 搔

chin [tʃɪn] 名 下巴

'Wrong!' said Jack. 'He dropped them all into the river. The bandits roared with **rage**. They called to Tashi to **mind** the horses. Then they jumped into the water and tried to **recover** the bags of rice that were **sinking further** down the river.'

「錯了！」傑克說。「他把袋子全丟進河裡。強盜們氣得大吼大叫。他們叫大喜照料馬匹。接著他們便跳進河裡，想要救回漸漸沉到河裡的米袋。」

rage [redʒ] 名 勃然大怒

mind [maɪnd] 動 照料

recover [rɪˋkʌvɚ] 動 拿回

sink [sɪŋk] 動 下沉 《down》

further [ˋfɝðɚ] 副 再往前地

'But Tashi reached them first, I suppose,' said Dad.

'No, he didn't,' said Jack, 'and when the bandits came back, all angry and **dripping**, they found that he had lost all the horses. The robbers began to whisper about the Bandit Wife, and Me Too gave Tashi **evil** looks. It took them a whole day to find the horses again.

「不過，我猜大喜先拿到了米袋。」老爸說。

　　「不，他沒有，」傑克說，「強盜們回來的時候，全都又溼又氣，他們發現大喜把馬匹全弄丟了。強盜們開始在背後說強盜婆子的壞話，而密圖兇惡地瞪著大喜。他們花了一整天的時間去把馬找回來。

dripping [ˋdrɪpɪŋ] 形 溼透的
evil [ˋivl̩] 形 邪惡的

'Well, that night, the Bandit Chief said to his wife, "This boy is not like our son. He sings like a crow, he tangles your hair, he loses the rice and **scatters** the horses." Tashi put on a sorrowful face. "I will do better tomorrow," he promised.

'"You'd better," whispered Me Too, "or I'll **pluck** out your nose hairs, one by one."

「嗯，那天晚上，強盜頭頭跟他老婆說，『這小子不像我們兒子。他的歌聲像烏鴉一樣難聽，讓妳的頭髮打結，弄丟了米，還放走了馬匹。』大喜做了一個難過的表情。『我明天會做得更好的，』他保證。

　　「『你最好這樣，』密圖低聲地說，『否則我就一根一根拔掉你的鼻毛。』

scatter [`skætɚ] 動 驅散

pluck [plʌk] 動 拔

'On the third day, the bandits decided to **attack** the village where another band of robbers were staying. Just before **dawn** they quietly surrounded the camp—and what do you think Tashi did then?'

'He rode into the village and captured the chief,' guessed Dad.

「第三天，強盜們決定去攻擊別幫盜匪落腳的村子。就在天亮前，他們靜悄悄地包圍了那個營地——你想大喜做了什麼？」

　　「他騎馬進村子，逮住了對方的頭頭，」老爸猜。

attack [ə`tæk] 動 攻擊

dawn [dɔn] 名 黎明

'Wrong!' cried Jack. 'They were just preparing to attack, when Tashi **accidentally let off** his gun.

'The **enemy** was **warned** and Tashi's bandits had to **gallop** away for their lives.

「錯了！」傑克大聲說。「就在他們準備要進攻的時候，大喜恰巧開了一槍。

　　「敵人收到了警告，大喜那幫強盜只好快馬加鞭地逃命了。

accidentally [ˌæksəˈdɛntḷɪ] 副 碰巧

let off 開（槍）

enemy [ˈɛnəmɪ] 名 敵人

warn [wɔrn] 動 警告

gallop [ˈgæləp] 動 （騎馬）飛奔

When they were at a safe distance they stopped. The Chief's brother wanted to punish Tashi—he said he'd tie him up and **smother** him in honey and let man-eating ants **loose** upon him—but the Bandit Wife said, "No, let him come back to camp with me. He can help me **roast** the ducks we stole yesterday and we will have a **feast** ready for you when you return."

'So she and Tashi worked all day, plucking, chopping and turning the ducks on the **spit**, and mouth-watering smells greeted the bandits as they drew near the camp that evening. And what do you think Tashi did then?'

當他們安全了以後，就停了下來。密圖想處罰大喜
——他說，他要把大喜綁住，把蜂蜜厚厚地塗在他身上，
接著把食人蟻放上去——但是，強盜婆子卻說，『不，讓
他跟我一起回去營地。他可以幫我烤昨天偷來的鴨子，
我們會在你們回來之前，把酒菜準備好。』

「所以啦，她和大喜便忙了一整天，又拔毛又剁肉，
還把鴨子叉起來轉啊轉、烤啊烤的。那天晚上，強盜們
快回到營地的時候，那令人垂涎三尺的香味歡迎著他們。
你想大喜接著做了什麼？」

smother [`smʌðɚ] 動 厚厚地覆蓋住
loose [lus] 動 放
roast [rost] 動 烤
feast [fist] 名 美食
spit [spɪt] 名 （烤肉用的）叉

'Washed his hands for dinner,' said Dad.

'Wrong!' said Jack. 'Just as the robbers jumped down from their horses, Tashi **stumbled** and **knocked** a big pot of cold water over the almost-cooked ducks and **put out** the fire.

「他洗洗手準備吃晚餐，」老爸說。

「錯了！」傑克說。「就在強盜們跳下馬的時候，大喜跌了一跤，將一大桶的冷水踢翻在快烤熟了的鴨子上，還把火澆熄了。

stumble [ˋstʌmbl̩] 動 絆倒

knock [nɑk] 動 撞上

put out 熄滅（火）

'"Enough!" shouted the Bandit Chief to his wife. "This boy is not like our son. He sings like a crow, he tangles your hair, he loses the rice, he scatters the horses, he warns our enemies—and now he has **spoilt** our dinner. This is too much."

「『夠了！』」強盜頭頭對他老婆大喊說，『這小子根本就不像我們兒子。他歌唱得像烏鴉，讓妳的頭髮打結，弄丟了米，放走了馬匹，還警告我們的敵人——現在他毀了我們的晚餐。太過份了。』然後他轉向大喜。

spoil [spɔɪl] 勔 毀掉

"You must go home to your village now, Tashi. You are a **clumsy**, useless boy with no more **brain** than the ducks you **ruined**."

'Tashi smiled inside, but he put on a sorrowful face and turned to the Bandit Wife. "I'm sorry that I wasn't like your son," he said, but she was already on her way down to the river to **fetch** some more water.

「『你現在得回你的村子了，大喜。你這個又笨又沒用的小子，比那些被你毀掉的鴨子還沒大腦。』

　　「大喜心裡偷笑著，不過卻裝出一副很難過的表情，轉身向強盜婆子說，『我很難過我不像你兒子，』不過她已經往河邊提水去了。

clumsy [`klʌmzɪ] 形 笨手笨腳的

brain [bren] 名 頭腦

ruin [`ruɪn] 動 破壞

fetch [fɛtʃ] 動 取來

'Tashi turned to go when a **rough** hand pulled him back.

'"You don't **deserve** to go free, Duck Spoiler," **snarled** Me Too. "Say goodbye to this world and hello to the next because I'm going to make an end of you."

「當大喜轉身要走的時候，一隻粗暴的手把他拉了回來。

　　「『哪有這麼容易就放你走，毀了鴨子的小鬼，』密圖大吼大叫。『跟這個世界說再見，準備下地獄吧，因為我要宰了你。』

rough [rʌf] 形 粗魯的
deserve [dɪ`zɝv] 動 應得
snarl [snɑrl] 動 大吼大叫

'But as he turned to pick up his **deadly** nose-hair plucker, Tashi shook himself free and **tore off** into the forest. He could hear the bandit **crashing** through the trees after him, but if he could just make it to the river, he thought he would have a chance.

「不過就在他轉身去拿那把可以致人於死地的鼻毛夾時，大喜甩開了他，拔腿跑進森林裡。他聽見那強盜硬踩過森林追趕他的聲音，不過如果他可以去到河邊，他想他會有機會逃跑的。

deadly [`dɛdlɪ] 形 致命的

tear off 迅速離開

crash [kræʃ] 動 強行前進

'He was almost there when he heard a **splash**. He looked up to see the Bandit Wife had **slipped** on a stone and had fallen into the water.

"'Help!" she cried when she saw Tashi. "Help me, I can't swim!"

「就在他差不多到河邊的時候，他聽見撲通一聲。他抬頭一看，看到強盜婆子在石頭上滑了一跤，掉進水裡了。

　　「『救命啊！』她看見了大喜，大聲喊叫。『救救我，我不會游泳！』」

splash [splæʃ] 名 濺水聲

slip [slɪp] 動 滑倒《on》

'Tashi **hesitated**. He could **ignore** her, and
dive in and swim away. But he couldn't leave
her to **drown**, even though she was a bandit.
So he swam over to her and pulled her **ashore**.

'By now all the bandits were **lined** up along the
bank and the Chief ran up to Tashi. "Thank you,
Tashi. I take back all those hard words I said
about you. **Fate** did send you to us after all."

「大喜猶豫了一會兒。他大可以不理她，跳進水裡，游泳離開。不過即使她是一個強盜，他也不能讓她淹死。於是他向她游了過去，把她拉上岸。

hesitate [`hɛzə,tet] 勳 猶豫

ignore [ɪg`nɔr] 勳 不理睬

dive [daɪv] 勳 跳水 《in》

drown [draʊn] 勳 淹死

ashore [ə`ʃɔr] 副 往岸上去

「這時所有的強盜沿著河岸排成一列，頭頭跑向大喜。『謝謝你，大喜。我收回之前對你所說的一切重話。終究是命運把你送來給我們的。』

line [laɪn] 動 排成一列 《up》

fate [fet] 名 命運

'Me Too **groaned** and **gnashed** his teeth.

'"Brother," said the Bandit Chief, "you can see Tashi safely home."

「密圖哼了哼，咬牙切齒。
『老弟，』強盜頭頭說，『你把大喜平安送回家。』

groan [gron] 勔 發出哼聲
gnash [næʃ] 勔 咬（牙）

'"Oh no, thanks," said Tashi quickly, "I know the way," and he nipped off up the bank of the river, quicker than the wind.'

「『哦，不用了，謝謝，』大喜趕忙說，『我認得路的，』接著他跑得比風還快，一溜煙便從河岸上跑走了。」

'So,' said Dad sadly, 'that's the end of the story and Tashi arrived safely back at his village.'

'Wrong!' said Jack. 'He did arrive back at the village and there were great **celebrations**. But at the end of the night, when everyone was going sleepily to bed, Third Uncle noticed that a ghost-light was shining in the forest.'

「所以，」老爸依依不捨地說，「故事就這樣結束了，大喜安全回到他的村子了。」

　　「錯了！」傑克說。「他是回到了村子裡，而且大大地慶祝了一番。不過，很晚很晚的時候，正當大夥兒都要回去睡覺了，三叔注意到樹林裡有鬼火在閃爍。」

celebration [ˌsɛləˈbreʃən] 名 慶祝

'And that's another Tashi story, I'll bet!' cried Dad.

'Right!' said Jack. 'But we'll save it for dinner when Mom gets home.

「我敢說，那一定是大喜的另一個故事囉！」老爸喊了起來。

「沒錯！」傑克說。「不過，我們要把這個故事留到老媽回家吃晚餐的時候再說。」

專為青少年朋友設計的百科全書

人類文明小百科

行政院新聞局推介
中小學生優良課外讀物

人類文明小百科，全套共十七冊

為臺灣的新生代開啟一扇知識的窗

歐洲的城堡

法老時代的埃及

羅馬人

希臘人

希伯來人

高盧人

樂　器

史前人類

火山與地震

探索與發現

從行星到眾星系

電　影

科學簡史

奧林匹克運動會

音樂史

身體與健康

神　話

小普羅藝術叢書

·小畫家的天空系列·

活用不同的創作工具

靈活表現各種題材

讓青少年朋友動手又動腦

創造一個夢想的世界

國家圖書館出版品預行編目資料

大喜與強盜 / Anna Fienberg,Barbara Fienberg著;Kim
　Gamble繪;王秋瑩譯.－－初版一刷.－－臺北市;
　三民，民90
　　面;公分--(探索英文叢書.大喜說故事系列;4)
中英對照
ISBN 957-14-3414-0　(平裝)
　1.英國語言—讀本

805.18　　　　　　　　　　　　　　90002838

網路書店位址　http://www.sanmin.com.tw

ⓒ　大 喜 與 強 盜

著作人　Anna Fienberg　Barbara Fienberg
繪　圖　Kim Gamble
譯　者　王秋瑩
發行人　劉振強
著作財　三民書局股份有限公司
產權人　臺北市復興北路三八六號
發行所　三民書局股份有限公司
　　　　地址 / 臺北市復興北路三八六號
　　　　電話 / 二五○○六六○○
　　　　郵撥 / ○○○九九九八——五號
印刷所　三民書局股份有限公司
門市部　復北店 / 臺北市復興北路三八六號
　　　　重南店 / 臺北市重慶南路一段六十一號
初版一刷　中華民國九十年四月
編　號　S 85582
定　價　新臺幣壹佰柒拾元
行政院新聞局登記證局版臺業字第○二○○號

ISBN　957-14-3414-0　（平裝）